It's
Bumpy
at the
Back
of the Bus

Kimberly Prey

ISBN: 978-1-954095-10-6

It's Bumpy at the Back of the Bus

Yorkshire Publishing

1425 E 41st Pl

Tulsa, OK 74105

www.YorkshirePublishing.com

918.394.2665

Published in the USA

This book belongs to:

· ·

I have something important
that we must discuss.

I've heard that it's bumpy
at the back of the bus!

I tried to sit up
front one day...

But not even one bump
came my way.

I tried sitting in the middle...

But I didn't even feel
a tiny jiggle.

When I finally made it to the back of the bus...

I was ready to see if it was worth all the fuss!

Here is a city street!

My legs fly off the seat!

Bumpity

Bumpity

BUMP!

I see a train track!

A crazy tickle rolls
down my back!

Bump-a
Bump-a
Bump!

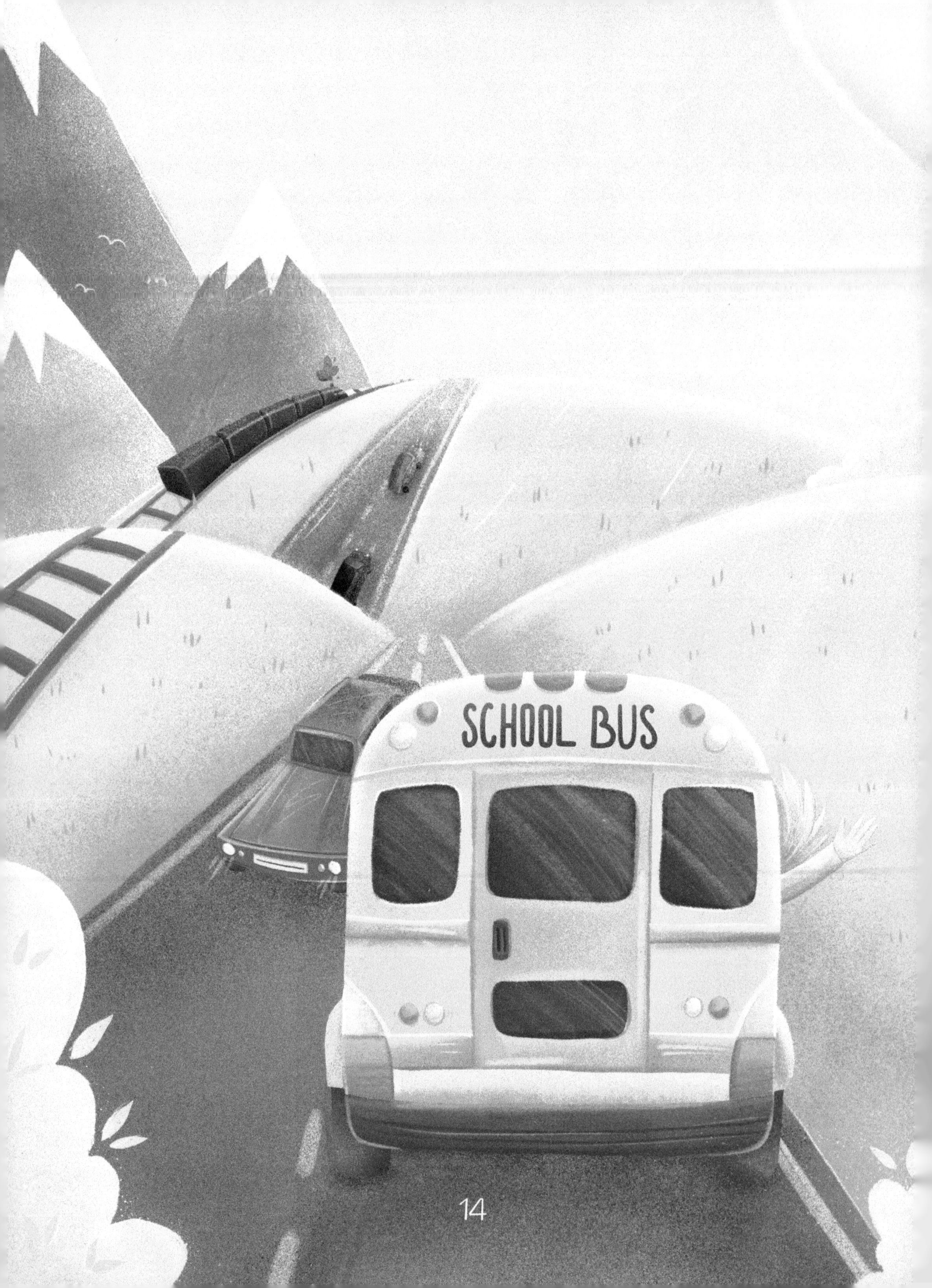
SCHOOL BUS

The bus is moving
to the highway!

My hair feels like it
might fly away!

Zoomy

Zoomy

Bump!

A country road covered
in dust is here!

I grin with excitement
from ear to ear!

Bumpeeeee
Bumpeee
Bump!

Finally, a fast curve
is what I see!

I shout out a big

WOW

WHEEEEEE!!!!

Ka-bump

Ka-bump

KAAAA-BUMP!

Oh back of the bus...
I will always love
every bump!

Those amazing bumps make
my heart happily jump.

Jump!
Jump!
BUMP!

9 781954 095106